# Burning Windows

# Burning Windows

by Zach Cook
illustrated by Wanda Wilson

**Burning Windows**
Copyright ©2024 by Zach Cook
Illustrations copyright ©2024 by Wanda Wilson

Author: Zach Cook
Illustrator: Wanda Wilson

All rights reserved. No part of this publication may be reproduced, stored in a retrieval system, or transmitted in any form or by any means - for example, electronic, photocopy, recording - without the prior written permission of the publisher. The only exception is a brief quotation in printed reviews.

The opinions expressed by the author are not necessarily those of Bell Asteri Publishing & Enterprises, LLC.

Published by Bell Asteri Publishing & Enterprises, LLC
209 West 2nd Street #177
Fort Worth TX 76102
www.bellasteri.com

Published in the United States of America

ISBN: 978-1-957604-21-3 (hardback)
ISBN: 978-1-957604-22-0 (paperback)

# Author's Note

When I was nine years old, my little brother was diagnosed with leukemia. I struggled with processing his diagnosis, so I learned to suppress my emotions for many years as he recovered. I wanted to be a shoulder to lean on for my brother, family, and those around me at all times. I worked tirelessly to keep a strong image intact until I realized the power of letting *the fire* out. Everyone has different ways of processing life's challenges, but for me, it was by setting my thoughts free through short stories and poetry. *Burning Windows* is a chronological collection of my favorite pieces I've written from ages 17 to 20. It displays a gradual rise in maturity and paints a shift from childhood to adulthood. It is intended for anyone who has ever felt alone in their struggles and suggests the question: "Should I *open up the windows and let my fire out too?*".

Each page includes a small sketch illustrated by my grandmother, Wanda Wilson. She is living proof that there is light at the end of the tunnel for anyone searching for hope.

All of the proceeds of this book will be donated to Active Minds in hopes for a future with increased mental health awareness and education. You can visit their website by scanning the QR code below.

# Burning Window

The stars felt
Like fireballs
From behind the glass pane

So every night,
I pulled forth the curtain
In fear of light on my face

And then all of a sudden
On one blue, boiling night
I decided to let them
Beam their fiery light

So I reached for the window,
My hands shaking with fear,
And I unlatched the notches
That I'd kept sealed for years

And then all of a sudden
On that bright, beaming night
I felt an angry house fire
Throw itself to the sky

So if anyone was watching
From the depths of that dusk,
They'd find a man
Behind his burning windows

They'd watch him finally realize
That the source of the heat
Was not from others' eyes,
But a furnace beneath

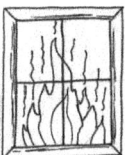

# Supernova

My star doesn't shine like she used to.
She once wore pink
And frilly bows
Had glitter eyes
A rhinestone nose

But now she cries
When she's alone
Her diamond smile
No longer gold

As sunsets fade
Her pink retires
Replaced with black
Her heart hard-wired

I miss her gleam
My sweet spring flower
But all stars die
Meteor shower
My star doesn't shine like she used to.

# My Poltergeist

When the headlights clear
And the burnouts fade
I'm left alone with fear,
My fragile mind contained.

And now it's lights out
You come to visit me
You found the right route,
Crept up the cyprus tree.

Tap at my windowpane
I hear the raven's crow
I feel your shadowed frame,
Stealing the moon's faint glow.

I listen to your nails
Shrill grinding at my door
And as I try to wail,
You slide across my floor.

I wish that I could run
But I can't move a thing
Oh how I miss the sun,
Replaced by your tight cling.

Now I can feel your breath
It's cold as polar ice
You fill my room with death,
My friend, my poltergeist.

# The Party

A ghostly echo
Of light and fulfillment
Refracts off the red brick rouge
The house teems with brilliance
From the street

It vibrates through the soles of my
Lake stained high tops
I drift into the dark
Splashing through the sparks
I'll die before
I fall apart
In their arms

# The Essence of Dawn

It's half past five and
The fresh day
Has just begun

Even the jays and
Finch don't fray
For the war is done

The dawn boasts hope and
Peace today
The sun will surely come

# Youthful Voice

The phonograph
Has never seemed
So dull.

Her bones are thrashed,
Mahogany bashed,
So I've been told.

But look,
Draw close,
For melodies she sings.
Your ears,
Her ring,
Prove age is not a thing.

# Green Eyes

They say green eyes
Are of the rarest kind
But blue,
The sky,
The sea,
Nice try!

They say green eyes
Hold the colors of spring,
But brown,
So deep,
So wise,
I scream!

They say we all
Get our chances to lead
But I
Can't see
The green eyes
In me.

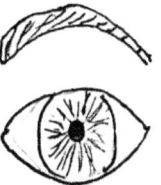

# Touch of an Angel

He finally touched the sky.
His soul is safe
From the wretched wraiths
For he finally feels the sky.

He's living with the suns.
The fire and glow
Of freshly laid snow
Summer and ice, his new home
For he is dancing with the suns.

Through prayer I feel his touch.
The angels and
The holy bands
Lift him from this tattered land
And hold him with maternal hands
For God has gifted me his touch.

I will always feel
Your touch.

# The Old Bay

You laugh in my face
While I deepen your hue
You've made a mistake
I know I've made a few

Your garden so thick
Through weeds I will crawl
We felt the rose pricks
Now our petals will fall

# The Sailboat

The tiny sailboat
Faces the
Long storm
His hull stays afloat
But his sails are
Long torn

# Is It Worth It?

A massive multicolor
Waste of time
They clink their glasses
You're flying by

Aren't you tired
Of showing up?
The more you give them
The more they want

Like a mosquito
They suck your blood
You're slipping slowly
At least you're fun

# Sycamore Street

A blur of light
And nostalgia
Blanket
Sycamore Street.

From chasing
The dogs
To driving
Shiny new cars
The memories sustain.

We move on,
We spread our wings
And fly off.

But Sycamore Street
Stays in our hearts.

# The Tree of Life

Sweet candy fruits
And honeysuckle
Wrap the shoulders
And the thighs

A thousand twisting
Branches
One hundred
Fireflies
An inferno of
Your beauty

You laid down
To bring me
Life

# This City

The metro bus
Screeches to a halt
And a flood
Of strangers
Gushes onto the pavement

Bloodshot eyes
Reflect their only hopes
They're liking posts
As the world
Succumbs to flames and anarchy

Like the worker bee
They click and clack
Then time stops.
But it's too late
To water the concrete

# From the Rooftop

From the
Rooftop
The world burns a little
The heat
Rises
And steam stings the sky

Amidst
The smog
Our moon sweetly smiles
Beaming
With lies
And bursts of denial

We're laughing,
You're leaving,
Your light's
So deceiving.
Through screaming
And crying
You smile
in the fire.

# The Night Train

A steady crimson beats
On the rusty rails
Of yesterday

The luster of the
Night train
Gleams its way
Into tomorrow

The traveling circus
And the sturdiest of stallions
The high school band
And a symphony of thousands

From crocheting crones
To the newborn infant
The night train
Holds the world

Held by time
And the fall of dusk
We all sleep the same
We're all made of dust

So why do we fight
When we could love?

It's time we link
Our arms as one
To love our neighbors
Like our sons,
For we all ride
The same night train
into the same setting sun.

# Dreaming

Pinch me
For I know
I will desperately
Miss this moment

Awake me
For the color
In my eyes
Will be gone
By the morning

# Castaway

I put my
Heart on a
Fishing hook
And I
Cast it
Out to sea

Piece by piece
Its robbed
From me
But I
Love it

But I love it

# Stanzas

So I
Shoved
My years
Into stanzas
And the
Pages
Set me
Free

# Fireflies

Together
We glowed
Like two
Fireflies
In a jar
Made of
Crystal

# Citrus Tree

Last year
I made
lemonade
And carefully
Picked
A seed
From the citrus

With a plastic
Beach shovel
I tucked
The seed
Into a bed
Of soil and roses
And hoped

Now lemons
And success
Offset the
Red bush
And I
Bask in
The shade of
A magnificent tree

# **Pinwheel**

Like a
Pinwheel
I'll spin
Forever

Trying to
Be the best

Maybe
One day
I'll fly
Off the axel

And cease
The never ending
Cycle

# Broken Mirrors

I smashed
A mirror
And watched
The shards
Trickle down
The sink

I'll take
The bad luck
As long as I
Never have to
See that
Man
Again

# Candlesticks

I lit my fingers on fire
Like candlesticks

Then I touched your face
So we could

Burn together

# Cigarette Stars

I handed
You a star
And you smoked
It like a
Cheap cigarette

Now I
Don't give out stars,
For your craving
Stole them all

# Faraway Umbrella

The sky is crying
Like he has
Lost his greatest
Love

He asked me
To stay up with
The barn owls
To craft you
An umbrella

So I ripped up
My best coat
And searched
For my finest
Silver

Because he knew
I wouldn't be there

But my love
Will shield you
From the darkest
Storms

# Lost in the Gold Rush

I have been
Searching
For gold

When I should
Have been happy
With my silver

# Broken Homes

I built a house
Up in the clouds.
I painted the skies,
But as time flies,

Its sturdy bones
Begin to fold.
Its bricks turn to gray
While the floorboards
All fray.

# Dusk's Lullaby

While the
June bugs
Kiss
My headlights

I sink into
The cold
Leather
And I get lost
In the
Sounds
Of the night

# Embers

We built this home
To watch it fall
From the neighbor's yard
We felt it all

As embers drift
Down the boulevard,
Our eyes lock
And we do it all again.

# Overstimulation

I bite my nails
As the bar music
Gets so loud
I can't breathe

The dingy bricks
Close in
And I slip into
The dark abyss

# Godspeed

When I drive
I like to dream
That my wheels
Can tread air

And my gears
Run on prayer
As the wind
Sparks a flare

I look to Heaven

Take the wheel
Take me there

# Arctic Heart

I held you
Like an otter
Holds a clam
In the ice

But unlike
The arctic
The ice
Came from you

While I kept
You warm
You kept
Me blue

And slowly
You froze
My bones
From the outside in

# Mustang

You're a
Cherry red
Mustang

Nothing can
Stop you
For you don't
Seem to care

But when the
Dead end hits
You'll be all alone

Sometimes it
Takes a rough crash
To mend a
Lost soul

# Living Pond

I once was
A pond
Full of life

Lilies and
Tadpoles
Filled my veins
And amber
Ducklings
Skimmed
My mind

But then you came
And sucked me dry
Now all that's left
Is stone and grime

# Scrapes

I scraped
My elbow
When I was ten
And laughed it off
So I wouldn't cry

I've been laughing
Things off
Since then
And my soul
Can't keep up
With all this
Suppression

# Fragility

A sparkling
Dragonfly
Surfs on
Sun rays
And glides
From tree to tree

So careless
And fragile
Such a
Breathtaking
Green

So wild
And blatant
And charming
And free

# Front Line

Like a soldier
I'll stand
At the front
Of the line

I'll take all
The bullets
And smile
In the flames

Yet I still ask
For mercy
An escape
From the pain

# Swan Lake

Two white swans
Glide through
The pond

Their tangerine
Feet push on
Through the moss

No thing
Could disrupt
Their dwindling grace

Two heart beats
Live on
And haunt the blue lake

# Lovestains

Like the
Grass stains
On my
Favorite denim

You're stubborn
And you stick
Like honey
To feathers

# Poisoned

I've been living
In this chemical state
For so long
That my blood
Has turned
To poison

Why do I stay?

Maybe because
The sting
Is slow and sweet
Like molasses

# Stuck in the Woods

I rued the hour
That night fell
For every ghost
Shook every elm

And icy frost
Rained down on me
Then haunting hail
Slipped from the leaves

So there I sat
Within the bush
And felt my soul
Escape the woods

# Lanterns

I want to
Glow like
The lanterns
In Chinatown

Every orb
Bringing hope
To the children
Of the night

Every hue
Of the summer
Burning through
Winter's bite

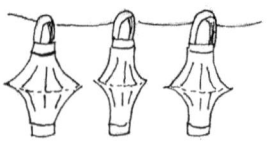

# 1,000 Lifetimes

You ask me
If you will be okay

And time stops

These four walls
Won't hold you
Forever, I hope

I say, "I cannot
Foresee the future
But I know

That you deserve
One thousand
Lifetimes"

# The Lost Kingdom

I miss when
You made me feel
Like I was the ruler
Of my own
Little kingdom

I loved those days,
But now I've learned
That little kingdoms
Never last

# Hospitable Moments

Holding your
Little hand
As the machines
Start a riot
And the screens
Beep for miles

I feel as if
You are lost
In this sea
Of white tiles

But then you
Awake
With those eyes
Like two lakes
And I remember
You are too strong
To leave us

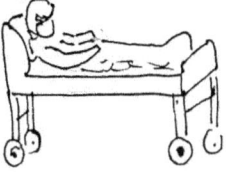

# Life's a Beach, Right?

If life is a beach,
Then it's one with
Red tide that reeks,
Stinging jellies,
And gray gulls that scream

If life is a beach
Then there's crabs
That pinch feet
And huge sharks
With white teeth

But if life is a beach
Still it's one we
Must see
Because a life on
The rocks
Can't compare
To the sea

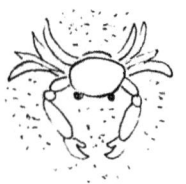

# Building Blocks to Acceptance

When I
Laid these
Bricks in
The mud
I had so
Many dreams
For a
Beautiful home

While this
Home is not
Beautiful
I have built
It myself

So I
Take a step back
And I accept
Every crack

# A Place We Call Our Own

I used to
Sit by the
The dam
On the west side
When life felt
Out of control

Somehow
The land felt
Untouched there
Like the grass
Had built
A home

Now as I
Speak to my
Reflection
And the
Bluegills below

I realize
I will miss
This place,
This place I call
My own

# Power of Ink

The world
Rests between
My index
And my thumb

The ink that
It bleeds
Has no limits
Or no walls

So I paint
The page blue
And hope my words
Live on and on

# Trapped Between Seasons

Fall has arrived
And the air is
Still heavy

The excitement
Of summer
Has faded

I'm alone, but not sad
In a trap
Between seasons

I prepare for the cold
As I fight to
Find reason

# Plato's Allegory

We live
Our lives
Watching shadows
On the walls

Why don't we face
The light
To see the world?

Maybe it's because
We don't want
To face
Reality

# Water Well

I slipped
Into a well
So deep
The moon's
Bright glow
Lost sight
Of me

But you
Saved me
From the
Darkest scene

When you filled
The hole
That swallowed
Me

# You Over Me

You know
I'm here
To take you
Home

Although
I'm tired
I face
The road

Under
Frosted
Skies and
Flaming snow

I'll make
Your bed
And then
Sleep cold

# City Longing

New York
Calls me
From my
Bay window

I close my
Eyes and feel
The vinyl seating
Of the yellow cab
On my thighs

The unfamiliar,
Familiar street
Scents are
Relentless now,
But somehow
Captivating

I want to go
To Manhattan
And be a face
In the crowd
Maybe then,
If I make it,
Maybe then
I'll be proud.

# Rebirth

I'm withering
Away as dusk
Floods across
The plains

I peer from the
Rocks while
My body melts
Into the limestone
And sediments below

The rebirth
Has begun
And the crimes
Of yesterday
Release
Like doves
From a casket

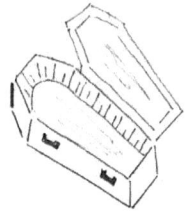

# Death of Memory

When we fall
And the sun
Hits our face
For the last time

Do our lives
Come undone?
Play on tape
For the skylines?

Or does time
Fade away
Will the reels
Float the shorelines?

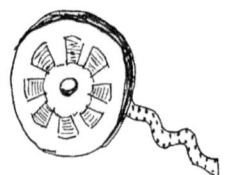

# Morning at the Harbor

Sunbeams
And coffee beans
The light comes
With harmony

The soft
Swallowtails
In willow trees
Flutter like sails
In seas of green

Watch the
Chemtrails
As the sailor sings
The dew is fresh
And light
Where the harbors meet

# All-Consuming Love

When love is
All consuming
It's like a
Grass stain
On denim
Or a blood drop
On linen

It never really fades
Never truly goes away
It only seeps into the seams
And burrows deep
Till it's unseen

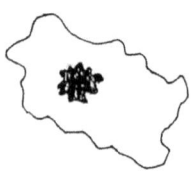

# Bayside Manor

Stately rows of white and gold
Frame the manor's deepest folds
From the bayside by the pier
One can see its primrose cheer

Sky blue like the warbler's crest
Linen drapes flow East and West
Each door freshly painted black
Glistens like a Cadillac

Rose blots ripple up the paths
Gracing stone with fiery glass
Daisies rest in lattice crowns
Dancing 'round like rolling clouds

From the bayside by the pier
One can smell the rot of tears
This time not the ocean's breath,
No, this salty air's from death

In the yard, so newly trimmed
A little mound of soil lives
And on that perfect mound one sees
A gravestone carved so tenderly

So when the lighthouse throws his beam
A mother weeps to fill the sea
The manor has seemed darkened since
That kingdom lost its little prince

# Love and the Fall

I held you in September
When autumn's burgeoning orange
First reached for the lowest limbs
And soft winds swept the highest hedges.

We lasted through October
When winter blew her first breath
And the orange had overtaken every oak
While we ran through its paint trail.

In November, when the orange was fading,
And shards of brown began to trace each leaf,
Our love grew defiant; it was headstrong,
And beautiful, but bludgeoning, and violent.

December ripped through the orange,
Handpicking each remaining leaf from every branch
And crumbling it under the weight of new snow,
Leaving an entire season of memories six feet below.

As you found new love in the coming winter,
I was left to mold with your past.

# Journey to Pride

Climbing the mountain has always been
The easiest part of the journey.
Reaching the peak and bathing in
The purest form of the sun is completely attainable.

Some might take pride in reaching the peak
And relishing in the valleys that they have overcome.
But that, the pride, is the part I will never understand.
What does it feel like? Is it a soft, tender hand?

Does it guide you along through treacherous lands?
I picture pride as a much stronger force,
Like a cougar, or bear, or a trained racing horse.
But I have not felt it, and I don't know its source.

When I reach the peak, and think back on my journey,
I say "It could have been faster if my legs weren't so weary."
"I shouldn't have fallen, my head is so hazy."
"With all of these scrapes, I have truly ashamed me."

I yearn to be proud, to embody the cougar,
But my heart is transfixed on my endless discrepancies.
I still fight to be proud, but it's a fixating battle,
So I'll bathe in the sun with these unbroken tendencies.

# Encircling Echoes

I miss when worries were simple,
And our hopes consisted of making our
Friends laugh, mastering our bicycles,
Or teaching the family dog how to spin in a circle.

As I have grown, my hopes have spun and twisted,
But unlike the family dog, they have circled endlessly.
They are no longer hopes, they are necessities.
They're more entrancing, like when you see something
That disgusts you, but you have to look since it's so interesting.

If I have learned anything from my seventeen years in this life,
It's that worries yearn to be embraced.
Each one will twist like a tornado until it spins so quickly
That the eye of the storm unveils a new one, one that
Is so much sharper and darker and unimaginably painful
That it replaces the old one.

Even after realizing this, I still
Dance around the eye of my tornado.
I form a hope, and I let it twist until I achieve it, and
When I don't, I cling on and let it twirl me into oblivion.

One day I will learn to stand in the eye of my storm,
To allow the worries to spin around me
Without spinning with them.

One day they will return to their origin, and become hopes again.
I guess I will spin until then.

# Treasure Hunting

His tiny, untouched fingers
Disappeared into the sand
As he pulled a broken clamshell
From the seaweed-ridden land

And like a tortured artist
He peered at it with intent
The glimmer in his green eyes
Turned to starlight as he grinned

With the mindset of a pirate
He began his daunting quest
He used pieces of the seashell
To form an orange colored X

In this moment I can see him
Digging deep only to find
There's no treasure at the bottom
Of his untouched little mind

Oh the things I'd do to stop him
From giving up this dream
As he sets down his blue shovel
And decides to finally leave

But the world put up a wall there
In between the boy and me
For it's a place with ill intentions
And sadly, still no time machine

# Unhealthily Whole

Bread and butter.
An unlikely pair, if you think about it.
Bread handcrafted with wheat from the soil,
And baked under heat to rise.

Butter, on the other hand,
Milked from a living cow and cultured,
Then placed in the cold to harden.
But then again, it is melted for bread.

People say opposites attract,
But I don't think that's always true.
Sometimes, like butter, one person is forced to conform,
For what is a stick of butter without heat to make it useful?

But at the same time, what is bread without butter?
It is plain and unexciting. It is expected to be bare.
But when the two meet, the bread does not change.
The butter is melted, but the bread stays the same.

Sometimes, when two people meet, and their origins
Are so incomparably dissimilar, the relationship is forced.
One person falls in love and conforms to the other,
Yet loses themselves in the process.

In this situation, the bread will never truly understand the butter,
Even though they work together to form something beautiful.
The "bread" will subconsciously suppress the "butter"
And together they will feel unhealthily whole.

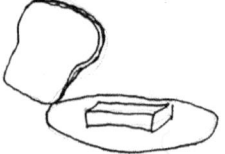

# Homesick

In the books and cartoons
We loved as children
The world is painted in a different light.

It is minimal yet drastic,
Simple yet complex.
It is a multicolor start and end,
Each chapter leading to a final resolution.

Yet as we grow,
The world begins to look differently.
Not because we see it in a new light,
But because we begin to notice the way it sees us.

So we mature, painstakingly shrouding
Our deepest longings and emotions,
Our fast-paced lifestyles leaving our souls
In constant states of disarray.

And as time progresses,
We forget about the endless possibilities
We once hoped our futures held,
Our imaginations crippled and cobwebbed.

If for one more day,
I could go back to being a child surrounded
By whimsical books and sugar coated cartoons,
I would cherish it with every single cell in my body.

Because now,
As I begin to accept this place for its darkness,
I find myself feeling home sick for a
Place that will never exist.

# Firefighter

I'm a firefighter
In the smoke
These burning bridges
Take me home

I like the smell
Of ash and coal
But as flames grow
I lose control

To fix my mess
I need a hose
I have to know
The water's close

And if the well
Runs dry as stone
I'll fill my pail
With melted snow

I'm a firefighter
In this smoke
But not by choice
It's in my bones

I have to know
I'm in control
Or else I'll burn
Or else I'll choke

# Violet

You taste brick and mortar
But you smell like sage
All the bitterness of licorice
With a voice like marmalade

Maybe if you'd let me peek
Inside that complex brain
I could help you understand
Why in august there's still rain

Acting in control, no doubt forcibly
For I see you in the shadows
Your eyes transfixed by memory
But Violet, what is it that you hide?

You suck me in your spiderweb
While you're singing lullabies
You're breathtaking, yet so hardened
Ruthless in disguise

But like the honey bee
Once you sting you'll surely die
You're draining yourself daily
When will your poison run dry?

# Illegible Eyes

Dark rust frames your gentlest features
A beauty so fragile and complex
That not even a looking glass could notice
The fault lines and splintering

Ruby and maroon like a dusk's haze in June
Circle your weathered, yet glistening eyes,
Resembling the intricacy of the burning bush,
I cannot read you, a quality I despise

Like dark wine and autumn clothing
You are intoxicating, yet so wise
A vintage leather driver's seat,
My metallic beauty with thrashed insides

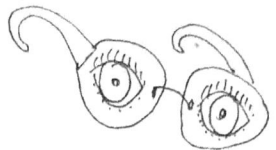

# Soul Fruit

Rip off each strawberry leaf
Tenderly so the fruit stays ripe
A sweet rouge drips from your fingers
Onto your ceramic little plate

You feel like a long time, no see
Fresh like cherries and oak trees
And as your teeth sink into my soul fruit
You form a chokehold within me

# Lost Silhouettes

Dusk eats away at Cannon Beach
And the road before us is long
So we dance with the pines by the shore
As the brightest star dies once again

It's the heartbreaks like this that last
The ones that sting like salt in the iris
The ones that leave you reeling in the dark
Your head slamming against green stone

It's the heartbreaks like this that burn
Silently fading love that laces the breath
Each word releasing new, hot emotions
As two silhouettes grow in comfortability

Sandy stains on my best white shirt
Remind me of the passion and longing
We left that night on Cannon Beach
Two lost silhouettes that no doubt,

Love and form light in another lifetime.

# Storm Chaser

If I close my eyes
And sink into the grooves
Of this rusty recliner
I can still hear the weather

Tap, tap on the windows
An ominous rain
Came flooding the sidewalks
On that ominous day

It ripped back the hedges
And smashed that old gnome
Those branches, they hugged us
While the dark ate our home

If I close my eyes
And hold out my right hand
I can still feel your cheekbone
As your face slips like sand

Tap, tap on my windows
Is that you at my door?
A swift glance at the doorway
Reveals it's just the storm

# Red Balloon

A little hand holds a red balloon
As it resists the raw wind
It violently dashes and cuts
Through the unforgiving autumn air

Five little fingers
Cling on to its string
But as the maple leaves form a tunnel
The balloon grows its wings

Suddenly, it's no longer resisting
It is soaring with grace
Like a ball from a cannon
It is destined to race

Over cars and bridges and old women's hats
Across hills and houses and those new shiny flats
Over the fair and the gardens and that old petting zoo
Across county lines it rises, slicing deep through the blue

But just before it takes the sun's hand
It gets caught in a power line
And grimly twists around wiry netting,
Terrified, the balloon bends and shakes

It searches for its home frantically
It yearns for a hand, those five fingers that will hold
But engraved in its nature,
It knows it can only move up from there

So it does.

Freedom is so awfully binding
For it is necessary to live freely
Yet so painstakingly difficult
When it means losing someone

I am a red balloon in this life
I find love, and I hold on so tight,
But when that little hand of love
starts to squeeze like a trap

I look to the sky and float off,
Just to later look back.

# Summer State

Spill that soda
Down your shirt
And laugh about it
Like you used to

I remember a time
When you laughed at mistakes
But now I watch you crumble
Even in the light of success

"What happened to the
Green grass behind that
Stone curtain," I ask.

"That green grass was
Never truly there.
It was just a patch
Of painted, wilting clovers,"
She mumbles.

"And when the time was right,
I let the rain wash all that
Green paint away."

And that's when I realized
We had a lot more in common
Than I could have ever imagined

Spill that soda
Down your shirt
But don't be afraid to break down
If it means you're being honest

# Smoke Signals

She lived by her own fire
Her hands forming patterns
Over the flames

She never left that fire unattended
It only festered and grew
As she violently tried to get us to notice

We didn't know it then
But she was sending smoke signals

We all saw her fire
But stayed too focused on our own
To realize hers was doused in gasoline

Eventually, her hands became scorched,
And we asked about her blisters,

But it was too late.

Our ignorance fueled her fire with a coal mine
And the flame had finally reached her soul

Now, we've learned to scream at sparks
And call out every tiny ember
For we have learned to watch for smoke signals
Since they first branded our hearts bitter

# Marmalade

In the little tan house
At the end of the street
There are three tiles in the kitchen
Weathered down by your feet

If I stand by the oven
I can still see you there
I can still hear you humming
Over boiling pears

You're smiling sweetly
As the steam rises up
Your white Texas hair
You tenderly tuck

And just like the records
That made your house home
Your hands spin like pinwheels
In a vast tornado

Your porch door is open
To the song of field crows
You're brushing back sweat beads
But it's "too nice to be closed"

Then you glance back at me
With those wise owl eyes
You gesture me over
As you toss in minced thyme

And from a steel hook
You grab a red apron
You drape it around me
My own cape made for stainin'

You hand me a citrus
Of bright orange hue
Then we chat about mandarins
While you peel back the fruit

Like a true southern chef
You add spice at your leisure
Throw a dash here and there
Since you never trust measures

With your trusty wood spoon
I help mix it together
You just stand back and smile
Your red lips stained like leather

In this delicate moment
I sense pride in your stare
Though it's not from our cooking
But the love that we share

All the honey of laughter
And your warm, tender care
Fill these walls made of plaster
Mending every small tear

And as Spring's sweet aroma
Dances on through the room
You then jar up our jumble
Of sugary stew

In the little tan house
At the end of the street
There's a jar in a cabinet
Filled with old memories

If I stand on those tiles
I can still feel the love
I would sell my own soul
For one last marmalade hug

# Lingering Luster

A table
For two
But there's
Only one

A delicate
Widow
Sits under
The sun

She's draped in
Blue silk
As the stone
On her finger

Reflects her
Whole life,
Its luster
Still lingers

# Nature's Roar

A hot gust
Of air
Tugs at
The oaks

The fruit bats
Scatter for
Shelter as the
Fierce lightning casts
Their fragile
Bodies into
Ferocious shadows

"A summer storm
Is brewing"
Scream the
Crickets

Then the clouds roar
And the woods
Come to life

# Rubix Cube

You remind me
Of a Rubik's Cube

Just when
I think
I've figured
You out,
A new color
Is revealed
And all of
My efforts
Become tangled

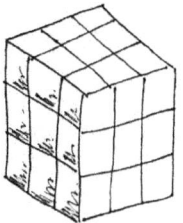

# Cityscapes

A rouge of
Shifting tail lights
Creep across
The highway

I would count
The constellations

But tonight,

The light pollution
Will do.

# Avalanches

Your smile
Is like
An avalanche

It crushes
And gleams
All at once

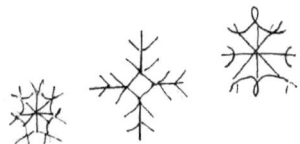

# Color Match

I'm a chameleon,
A never ending show.
Hand me your
Best colors

And I'll shift
To match their tone

I've been shifting
For a while,
Every day holds
A new coat

All this time
And all these layers
Make me weary
For a home

For what's the point
Of a chameleon
If his own green
Is never shown?

# Inheritance

The girl looked into the mirror
And wished hard for a new face
As her mother entered the room

Her mother noticed the girl's
Twisted brow
And tear stained jumper,
Seeing a younger version of herself.

With a gentle smile and a steady tone
The mother whispered,
"Your body is proof that your features
Have been cherished in past lifetimes."

And the daughter cried,
Because for a moment,
It all seemed real.

For a moment,
Her mother stepped out of the 4x4 frame
Above the splintering mahogany desk.

For a moment,
She could hear the soft hum
Of her mother's almost forgotten breath,
Each word dancing off the last and filling
The space with solace.

For a moment,
The girl yearned to see her mother
One last time.

To hold her and to show off her progress.
To feel her rough, yet benign fingertips
Trace her palm once more.
But most of all,
She yearned to thank her.

Because now,
As the girl looks into her mirror,
She doesn't see an oversized nose.
She doesn't cake lipstick over her thin lips
Or pluck the stray hairs her friends once
Called a unibrow.

She no longer sears her wavy hair
Into pin straight lines
And now finds gentleness in the
Brown eyes she once found boring.

Because now, as the girl
Stares at the reflection
She once despised,
She finds her mother staring right back.

And surely,
There is no inheritance
More valuable than that.

# Night Pricks

When the clock struck 12
And it was time to leave
All the night birds were peering
From their blistering trees.

And the long distance chatters,
Wistful wordings and stares,
Stung the back of my collar
As they prickled night air.

And the beams from the city
Slightly tainted the sky
From the edge of the forest
I could hear the streets cry.

In that dim, lonesome hour
Silence smoothed a blurred line,
And the colors of memory
Stained the dark night sublime.

Facing the night
Has always been so hard for me.
I despise being alone with my thoughts,
Having to face my future terrifies me.

But then I think of my past,
All the of the moments
I've created and cherished,
And I remember my true purpose:
To love and live, to make mistakes,
To fix them, and most of all,
To learn from the falls.

We're all just learning and living;
How incredible is it that we've been given that chance?

# Sparkshow

Everything goes black
As those emerald irises
Melt like a heat wave

Two dim bulbs before the light show

Then come the sparks from
Left and right
Around your collar
Painting the night

And come the sparks from
Past and present
Our hearts of brick
Turned soft in presence

It's all a red dusk before the moon glow

Then everything goes black
As I hold her for the last time
But I know that she'll be with me
When her sparks light up the skyline

# 433 Miles

There I was 433 miles away
A distance shared by two,
By two souls in foreign lands,
By two explorers that could love again.

There I was holding you from afar
Throwing all past direction to the winds,
My right hand reaching out for an invisible hand,
My left gripping the map to your heart.

There I was meeting new faces,
Trailblazing as I carefully built
A name for myself, a name for us.

But the heartstrings can only stretch
So far before they bust.

Now here I am 433 miles away,
Reading the letters you wrote me
As they start to fray like our memories.

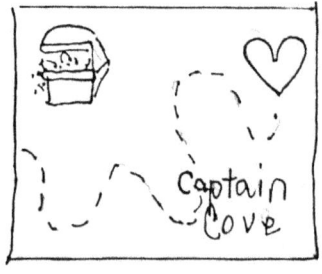

# Patinated Persons

If you look closely,
And I mean with precision,
Into the eyes of a stranger
With a life made on paper

You will see that their letters
Somehow bleed all together
That their face made of plaster
Is a lie that they've mastered

And I know it seems harsh,
But I know this for certain
For I am made of paper
For I am this lost stranger

And they think that I'm winning
But they can't know the truth
While I'm wasting away
In this endless pursuit

And I write this with passion
Since I need you to know
That the ones you compare with
Are patinated with gold

At the end of the day,
We're all from the same stone.
At the end of the day,
We're all fighting for hope.

# Darkest Sublime

From the railings of this villa
I can see the sailboats glide
All the people do their prancing
Under rouging purple skies

And they're holding on to lost love
While they're sinking in sublime
I wonder why the perfect people
Boast the darkest, saddest eyes

# Haunting Threads

Today I took the clothes
That somehow still remind of you
And I folded them into a pile
In the corner of my room

And there they hauntingly lay
Collecting dust each silent day
Living off time when love was easy,
When hands were held
And hearts were full

# Pursuit of Addiction

Have you ever watched a moth's journey to the light?
It starts with curiosity, the moth wandering close and then far.

Escalating into infatuation,
The moth will begin to brush the bulb
With its wings.

Feeling true heat for the first time,
The moth now lives for the touch of this light.
It breathes for the notion that it will one day
Join the bulb in its serendipity.

But like so many things in life,
The warmth comes with a consequence.

For the brave, little moth
Slowly sears at its own wings.

Like an addict with a passion,
It will never reach its dreams.

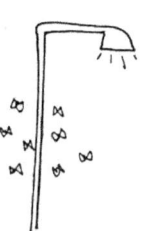

# Brainstorm

Sheets of blue rain down like the words
You screamed as you slammed my door.
You don't know it but I could love you more
And I wish you'd see that I've hit the floor.

Our dog years pass and I've watched them fly.
At this bus stop I can melt with time.
As our violent storm soaks into my mind,
I can pretend we've lived two separate lives.

And the rods of fire make me feel alive,
Reflecting light on strangers' darkened glares.
They see a child who wished he used his time
In finding love that didn't strip him bare.

I loved the way you'd brush your hair
Out of those eyes that used to care.
Out of the gray you held me there,
And as I drowned you simply stared.

Sheets of blue rain down like the words
You etched into my naive, tattered soul.
You don't know it, but I couldn't love you more,
Yet you'll never care that I have hit the floor.

# An Amber Introspection

As the solar reflection of gold amber
Paves its way across the hill country
I wonder if each valley has a meaning,
If each rock bottom moment holds value.

If the setting orb we call the sun,
The very thing that brings every tree life
And every withering weed hope,
Can reach each crevice of hidden terrain,
As far as any human eye can see,

Do we too have to touch the darkness to feel relief?

As the last remaining treetops fade to gray
And our burning ball of life hands its
Light to the blooming moon
The cycle of our inner psyche
becomes comically obvious.

We fall and get back up again, constantly,
Because the fall is what allows our eyes
To find the silver and gold linings
That frame every aspect of our complex lives.

# Heart of that House

Take me back to the heart of that house,
The one I grew up in.
I want to smell the cedar and sandalwood,
The scents of places that Dad's been.

Take me back to those four green walls,
The ones that nurtured a young mind.
I want to hear that weekend train,
The rusty wails that stopped all time.

Take me back to our herb garden,
Where I was taught the value of gentleness.
I want to chase the red birds,
The ones that sang of simple eloquence.

Take me back to the home I once knew,
To the house beyond physicality.
I don't miss the past for its memories,
But for my own individuality.

Take me back to myself,
To the mind before the comedown.
I yearn to hold the kid who dreamed
Of finding life beyond his hometown.

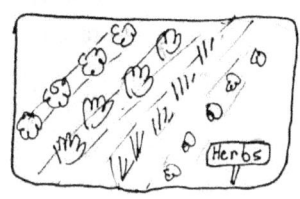

# Little Reflection

And there he was,
Begging for me to me to stay,
Yearning for someone to heal his wounds.

And there I was watching from above,
Ignoring his cries for help,
Leaving just as nightfall branded his soul.

I used to say my little brother was my polar opposite.
But now that I hold a mature set of eyes,
I see myself in every move he makes.

I see his burning passion to be the best.
I see the gentleness in his hand.

I watch him overthink his actions and
Hide his thoughts like shells in sand.

I watched his words tap at
My hardened exoskeleton,
His expressions reaching into my soul
And begging for a friend.

And I sat there,
Watching from above,
Too prideful to reach back.

Now, I find myself searching around corners,
Around streets and dark alleyways.
I find myself wondering why there's something missing.

And here I am,
Watching from below,
Alone and wishing I hadn't had been
So scared of holding my little reflection.

# Frostbite

As we held hands
For the last time
Our love froze at the surface
And you couldn't take it

My hands go cold
As the warmth
From your body
Dwindles too soon

You're colored violet
From the frostbite
Of my heart
And as I try to
Turn up the flame
Our skin slowly scars.

# A Blinded Waltz

And the waves gave way
As the wind brushed
Their whitecaps.

But the
Man in the moon
Burned like a gas lamp,

He wondered from above
Why he could not hold his work.
For the wind takes all the credit
For the lady in the sea,
Yet it pushes her around,
Forcing a love
That makes her weak.

He'll never waltz
With her like
The wind does,
For she is blinded
By the touch.

So night by night
He watches from afar,
A man expected to shine
With a dying wish to swim.

# Naive Yearnings

Like the gnat
Bouncing off
The flicker lamp

I live my life in
A pursuit of
Naive blindness

And so now I will
Touch the light I seek

To stop the world for
A second

To feel the heat
Of relief

# Quiet Strongholds

It's funny how the noise
Still dies out when I think of you

How the overlapping phrases
From the corners of
This coffee shop
Somehow drift
Up to the rafters

It's funny that only now,
I realize why I loved you

Because when I could not
Silence the noise
You were there
As a quiet stronghold,
One that I know I overlooked

And I think it's funny how now,
The noise I yearn for is not
Really a sound at all,

But a simple moment of your silence.

# Lessons From the Leaves

Canopy breath from that oak,
The one that somehow seems like
It's been burning for nine lifetimes,
Whips down leaves from the tree line.

And they twist like falling confetti,
Dotting blue with speckled jade

And they remind me of a time when
Life held more than judgment's gaze

For no one tells the leaves to soar,
In fact they're meant to hit the ground
And no one asks them to be sure
About their purpose in this town

So I think I'll take this time
To lose a little bit of grip
And learn a lesson from the leaves
To throw all worries to the wind

# About the Author

Zach Cook is a 20-year-old journalism student at The University of Texas at Austin. During his childhood in Houston, Zach became enthralled with the powerful influence of writing and decided early on that his life goal was to make a difference with words. In his free time, he enjoys being with friends, practicing the guitar, spending time with God, taking his dog on walks, playing sports, and especially, observing and documenting the detailed world around him. Zach is now striving to become a news anchor and hopes to continue authoring along the way. The ultimate goal of his work is to invite readers into a space where they feel understood and at peace within their own minds.

www.ingramcontent.com/pod-product-compliance
Lightning Source LLC
Chambersburg PA
CBHW070853050426
42453CB00012B/2169